ROTTEN RALPH

Helps Out

Written by Jack Gantos

Illustrated by Nicole Rubel

A Sunburst Book
Farrar, Straus and Giroux

For Mabel Grace —J.G.

For my family —N.R.

Text copyright © 2001 by Jack Gantos
Pictures copyright © 2001 by Nicole Rubel
All rights reserved
Distributed in Canada by Douglas & McIntyre Ltd.
Printed in December 2009 in China by South China Printing Co. Ltd.,
Dongguan City, Guangdong Province
First edition, 2001
Sunburst edition, 2004
5 7 9 10 8 6

Library of Congress Cataloging-in-Publication Data
Gantos, Jack.
    Rotten Ralph helps out / Jack Gantos and Nicole Rubel.— 1st ed.
       p.   cm.
    Summary: Sarah's cat Rotten Ralph tries to help her create a school project based
on ancient Egypt, but he is more of a hindrance than a help.
    ISBN: 978-0-374-46355-7 (pbk.)
    [1. Cats—Fiction. 2. Egypt—Civilization—To 322 B.C.—Fiction.
3. Homework—Fiction. 4. Schools—Fiction.] I. Rubel, Nicole. II. Title.

PZ7.G15334 Roh 2001
[E]—dc21
                                                                00-39405

The character of Rotten Ralph was originally created by Jack Gantos and Nicole Rubel.

Contents

Walk Like an Egyptian

One morning, Sarah was walking like an Egyptian.

She had been learning all about the ancient Egyptians for a big school project.

"Don't you think I look like Cleopatra, queen of the Nile?" she asked Rotten Ralph when he woke up.

Ralph was too hungry to care about Cleopatra or the Egyptians. He walked into the kitchen and smelled pancakes.

"Do you know where pancakes come from?" Sarah asked.

The store, Ralph said to himself.

"Ancient Egypt," Sarah said. "The Egyptians made the very first pancakes."

That's funny, Ralph thought. They don't taste old and moldy.

He burped loudly.

"Ralph!" scolded Sarah. "Mind your manners! Thanks to the Egyptians, you are not a wild animal."

Sarah informed Ralph that the Egyptians were the first people to have cats for pets.

If it were up to me, Ralph thought, it would be the other way around.

Sarah was going to the library to read more about Egypt for her school project.

"Ralph, I'm sure you can help me think of something great to build," she said. "After all, the ancient Egyptians believed cats were very wise and had special powers."

How about building a special litter box for *your* wise cat? Ralph suggested.

Sarah filled her red wagon with books to return to the library. She climbed in and asked Ralph to pull the wagon down the sidewalk.

"I bet you didn't know the Egyptians loved to ride in chariots," said Sarah.

I bet they didn't pull the chariots themselves, Ralph groaned.

Read Like an Egyptian

When they arrived at the library, Sarah told Ralph that the ancient Egyptians had libraries, too.

"People had to be quiet then," she whispered, "and they have to be quiet now."

It's as *quiet* as a tomb in here, Ralph thought.

"Ralph," said Sarah, "I want you to sit down and read this book on the pyramids. Maybe building a pyramid would be a good school project."

Sarah went to find a book about Cleopatra.

Reading about the pyramids gave Ralph big ideas.

He built a giant pyramid out of books.

"Ralph!" cried Sarah. "Books are not building blocks!"

Ralph jumped off, and the pyramid
crashed to the floor.

"Control yourself!" said the librarian.

"Now sit down and read," Sarah ordered. "You will like this book about mummies."

But Ralph's fur stood on end when he saw what Egyptians did to cats.

He crawled to the top of a bookshelf.

Sarah came running over.

"Ralph! Don't be a scaredy-cat. Come

down here and behave."

She gave Ralph another book.

"The Egyptians invented their own special kind of writing," she said. "They used pictures instead of letters."

She went to read more about how Cleopatra was the most powerful woman in Egypt. She had a huge army, and a palace filled with adoring cats.

The librarian caught Ralph writing all over the walls. She marched him over to Sarah.

"I'm sorry," she said, "but you and your naughty cat will have to leave."

Sarah was embarrassed. She
wondered if Cleopatra had ever been
this angry with one of her cats.

Shake Like an Egyptian

"Every time I want to do something fun, you spoil it," said Sarah when they returned home. "I wish you would learn how to help."

Ralph felt rotten.

He was ready to help.

He stuck out his paw.

"Okay, let's shake on it," said Sarah. "After all, the Egyptians invented the handshake."

"Maybe we should build a model of
an Egyptian boat?" Sarah suggested.

Rotten Ralph loved the idea and got
busy.

But he let the tub overflow and
began to float down the hallway.

"Ralph," cried Sarah, "please don't
flood the house!"

Sarah decided that building a desert
oasis might be better.

Ralph filled his wheelbarrow with
sand and made a pile in the living room.

He spread it around with a shovel.

He planted palm trees.

But Ralph's helping only upset Sarah.

He was making an Egyptian mess.

Then Ralph remembered his bug
collection. Sarah had said the
Egyptians loved beetles.

He ran to show his bugs to Sarah.
But he tripped over a palm tree.

Bugs landed all over Sarah's dress.

It was so disgusting she moaned out loud.

"I can't take your helping anymore!" she said.

35

"Ralph, you've been working so hard, why don't you go to bed early?"

Ralph yawned. Helping does make me tired, he thought.

While Sarah watched Ralph sleep, she felt bad for getting upset. Suddenly, she had a great idea.

Cleopatra loved cats just as I do, she thought. I should build a model of Cleopatra and her favorite cat.

She got some wire and twisted it into a shape. Then she made some papier-mâché and smoothed it over the wire.

Perfect! she thought. I will paint it
in the morning.

And she went to bed happy.

Look Like an Egyptian

Ralph woke up and saw what Sarah had made.

That doesn't look very special, he thought. Sarah still needs my help.

But when Sarah saw what Ralph had
done, she was not happy.

"Ralph!" she cried. "You've ruined
my statue of Cleopatra. Now I have
nothing for my project. My teacher is
going to be very disappointed."

Ralph hung his head. He had let
Sarah down again.

"What am I going to do?" said Sarah.
She went to her room to think.

Ralph did some thinking, too. Sarah and the Egyptians are right, he thought. Cats are very wise, and we do have special powers.

Ralph got busy all over again.

When Sarah saw what he was up to, she was thrilled. "Why didn't I think of this myself?" she said.

Ralph had dressed up as the Sphinx, the most famous Egyptian cat of all time. Sarah's teacher was impressed. Her school friends were impressed. Of course, Ralph was impressed with himself.

Sarah's classmates had good projects,
too. One showed how the Egyptians
invented checkers. One wore a big red
fez. One even charmed a garden snake
with an Egyptian flute. Sarah's teacher
praised all their work.

On the way home, Sarah wheeled
Ralph to the candy shop for a treat.

I love candy, Ralph thought.

"I know you do," Sarah said. "After
all, the ancient Egyptians were wise
enough to invent candy. And the
Sphinx is the wisest cat of all."